Dear Parent:

Congratulations! Your child is taking the first steps on an exciting journey. The destination? Independent reading!

STEP INTO READING® will help your child get there. The program offers five steps to reading success. Each step includes fun stories and colorful art. There are also Step into Reading Sticker Books, Step into Reading Math Readers, Step into Reading Phonics Readers, Step into Reading Write-in Readers, and Step into Reading Phonics Boxed Sets—a complete literacy program with something to interest every child.

Learning to Read, Step by Step!

Ready to Read   Preschool–Kindergarten
• big type and easy words • rhyme and rhythm • picture clues
For children who know the alphabet and are eager to begin reading.

Reading with Help   Preschool–Grade 1
• basic vocabulary • short sentences • simple stories
For children who recognize familiar words and sound out new words with help.

Reading on Your Own   Grades 1–3
• engaging characters • easy-to-follow plots • popular topics
For children who are ready to read on their own.

Reading Paragraphs   Grades 2–3
• challenging vocabulary • short paragraphs • exciting stories
For newly independent readers who read simple sentences with confidence.

Ready for Chapters   Grades 2–4
• chapters • longer paragraphs • full-color art
For children who want to take the plunge into chapter books but still like colorful pictures.

STEP INTO READING® is designed to give every child a successful reading experience. The grade levels are only guides. Children can progress through the steps at their own speed, developing confidence in their reading, no matter what their grade.

Remember, a lifetime love of reading starts with a single step!

Materials and characters from the movie *Cars 2*. Copyright © 2011 Disney/Pixar.
Disney/Pixar elements © Disney/Pixar, not including underlying vehicles owned by third
parties; and, if applicable: Pacer and Gremlin are trademarks of Chrysler LLC; Jeep®
and the Jeep® grille design are registered trademarks of Chrysler LLC; Porsche is a
trademark of Porsche; Sarge's rank insignia design used with the approval of the U.S.
Army; Volkswagen trademarks, design patents and copyrights are used with the approval
of the owner, Volkswagen AG; FIAT is a trademark of FIAT S.p.A.; Chevrolet Impala is
a trademark of General Motors. All rights reserved. Published in the United States by
Random House Children's Books, a division of Random House, Inc., 1745 Broadway,
New York, NY 10019, and in Canada by Random House of Canada Limited, Toronto, in
conjunction with Disney Enterprises, Inc.

Step into Reading, Random House, and the Random House colophon are registered
trademarks of Random House, Inc.

Visit us on the Web!
StepIntoReading.com
www.randomhouse.com/kids
Educators and librarians, for a variety of teaching tools, visit us at
www.randomhouse.com/teachers

ISBN: 978-0-7364-2807-1 (trade) — ISBN: 978-0-7364-8100-7 (lib. bdg.)

Printed in the United States of America 10 9 8 7 6 5 4 3 2 1

Random House Children's Books supports the First Amendment and
celebrates the right to read.

SUPER SPIES

By Susan Amerikaner

Illustrated by Caroline LaVelle Egan, Scott Tilley,
Andrew Phillipson, and Seung Beom Kim

Random House 🏠 New York

Lightning McQueen is
on a plane.
He is going
to a big race.

Mater is going,

too.

He will help Lightning.

Finn and Holley

are spy cars.

Bad cars try
to hurt race cars.
Finn and Holley
must stop them.

Holley calls Mater
at the race.

Mater likes Holley.

He leaves
to meet her.

Mater sees the bad cars.
Finn fights them!

9

Mater is not there
to help Lightning.
Lightning loses the race!

Lightning is mad
at Mater.

Mater wants
to go home.

The bad cars follow him
to the airport.
Finn will help!

Finn and Mater race away
from the bad cars.
Finn fights the bad cars.

Mater drives
into the spy plane.
Holley waits for him.
They will escape!

Holley and Finn
tell Mater
they are spy cars.

They think Mater
is a spy car, too.
Mater will help
find the bad cars.

Holley gives Mater
spy tools.
She dresses him up
to fool the bad cars.

Now Mater
is a spy car,
too!

Mater finds
the bad cars.

They want
to hurt Lightning!

Mater tries
to warn Lightning.
But Lightning does
not see him.

The bad cars catch
Finn, Holley, and Mater.
They trap them
in a big clock.

Mater gets away!

Holley escapes,
too!
She fights the bad cars.

Mater finds Lightning.
They race away
from the bad cars.

Mater uses
his spy tools.

He and Lightning
fly up
in the air.

Mater and Lightning

go to see

the Queen.

Mater helped
Finn and Holley
stop the bad cars.
The Queen thanks him.

Mater and Lightning

are heroes!

Dear Parent:
Your child's love of reading starts here!

Every child learns to read in a different way and at his or her own speed. Some go back and forth between reading levels and read favorite books again and again. Others read through each level in order. You can help your young reader improve and become more confident by encouraging his or her own interests and abilities. From books your child reads with you to the first books he or she reads alone, there are I Can Read Books for every stage of reading:

SHARED READING
Basic language, word repetition, and whimsical illustrations, ideal for sharing with your emergent reader

BEGINNING READING
Short sentences, familiar words, and simple concepts for children eager to read on their own

READING WITH HELP
Engaging stories, longer sentences, and language play for developing readers

READING ALONE
Complex plots, challenging vocabulary, and high-interest topics for the independent reader

ADVANCED READING
Short paragraphs, chapters, and exciting themes for the perfect bridge to chapter books

I Can Read Books have introduced children to the joy of reading since 1957. Featuring award-winning authors and illustrators and a fabulous cast of beloved characters, I Can Read Books set the standard for beginning readers.

A lifetime of discovery begins with the magical words **"I Can Read!"**

Visit www.icanread.com for information
on enriching your child's reading experience.

I Can Read Book® is a trademark of HarperCollins Publishers.

The Berenstain Bears Play Football! Copyright © 2017 by Berenstain Publishing, Inc. All rights reserved. Manufactured in China. No part of this book may be used or reproduced in any manner whatsoever without written permission except in the case of brief quotations embodied in critical articles and reviews. For information address HarperCollins Children's Books, a division of HarperCollins Publishers, 195 Broadway, New York, NY 10007.
www.icanread.com

Library of Congress Control Number: 2016944511
ISBN 978-0-06-235034-3 (trade bdg.) — ISBN 978-0-06-235033-6 (pbk.)

17 18 19 20 21   SCP   10 9 8 7 6 5 4 3 2 1
❖
First Edition

The Berenstain Bears® PLAY FOOTBALL!

Mike Berenstain

Based on the characters created by
Stan and Jan Berenstain

HARPER

An Imprint of HarperCollinsPublishers

It's time for football in Bear Country.

The Grizzly Bowl is on TV today.

The Bear family is having a Grizzly

Bowl party.

Family and friends gather at the
Bears' home.

There is a lot of food. There is a

lot to drink.

Everyone is talking and laughing.

Everyone is having a good time.

The TV is turned on for the game.

The cubs sit down to watch.

But there is just a lot of talking.

In between the talking,

there are a lot of ads.

"When does the game start?"

asks Brother.

"It doesn't start for hours yet," says Papa.

"They just talk about it first."

"Oh," says Brother.

The cubs are all bored.

They decide to go outside to play.

"What should we play?" asks Sister.

A football is lying on the grass.

"FOOTBALL!" everyone shouts.

The cubs choose teams.

They start to play.

Honey gets the ball.

She is small.

She runs between the other players' legs.

She scores a touchdown!

Now the other side has the ball.

They are all big.

They run right through the other players.

They score a touchdown, too.

Grizzly Gran is bored.

She is tired of all the talking on TV.

She is tired of getting food for everyone.

She looks out the window.

She sees the cubs playing football.

That looks like fun!

Gran goes outside.

"May I join you?" she asks the cubs.

"YAY!" the cubs shout. "Gran is going to play!"

Gran joins the team of Brother, Sister, and Honey.

"Now, here's my plan,"
whispers Gran.

Gran's team lines up.

"Thirty-three! Forty-four! Fifty-five!

HIKE!" yells Gran.

Brother hikes the ball to Gran.

Gran pretends to give the ball to Sister.

The other team follows Sister.

But Gran still has the ball.

She throws a long pass.

Brother catches it.

Touchdown!

Grizzly Gramps wants more food.

"Where's Gran?" he asks.

He sees her outside playing football.

"That looks like fun!" says Gramps.

He goes outside, too.

"Say," says Papa, "where's Gramps?"

He sees Gramps outside playing football.

"Hey, everybody!" he says.

"That looks like fun.

Let's all play!"

All the grown-ups go outside.

They start playing football.

They have a great time!

At last, the Grizzly Bowl comes on TV.

But there is no one to watch it.

Because they are all *playing* football.

Go team!